MICHAEL DAHL PRESENTS

GROSS GODS

MEDUSA and Her Oh-So Stinky Snakes

BY BLAKE HOENA
ILLUSTRATED BY IVICA STEVANOVIC

STONE ARCH BOOKS
a capstone imprint

Gross Gods is published by
Stone Arch Books
A Capstone Imprint
1710 Roe Crest Drive
North Mankato, Minnesota 56003
www.capstonepub.com

Library of Congress Cataloging-in-Publication Data
Hoena, B. A., author.
Title: Medusa and her oh-so-stinky snakes / by Blake Hoena.
Description: North Mankato, Minnesota : Stone Arch Books, a
    Capstone imprint, [2019] | Series: Michael Dahl presents: Gross
    gods | Summary: In this humorous (and gross) retelling of the
    Greek myth, Perseus and his disgusting friends set out to pluck
    one of the snakes from Medusa's head, before her baleful gaze
    turns them all to sludge.
Identifiers: LCCN 2019006161| ISBN 9781496583598 (hardcover) |
    ISBN 9781496584601 (pbk.) | ISBN 9781496583642 (ebook PDF)
Subjects: LCSH: Perseus (Greek mythological character)—Juvenile
    fiction. | Medusa (Greek mythology)—Juvenile fiction.
    | Mythology, Greek—Juvenile fiction. | Quests
    (Expeditions)—Juvenile fiction. | Humorous stories. | CYAC:
    Humorous stories. | Perseus (Greek mythological character)—
    Fiction. | Medusa (Greek mythology)—Fiction. | Mythology,
    Greek—Fiction. | LCGFT: Mythological fiction. | Humorous
    fiction.
Classification: LCC PZ7.H67127 Me 2019 | DDC 813.6 [Fic]—dc23
LC record available at https://lccn.loc.gov/2019006161

Design Elements: Shutterstock: Andrii_M, Anna Violet,
    Nikolai Zaburdaev

Designer: Tracy McCabe
Production Designer: Tori Abraham

MICHAEL DAHL PRESENTS

Michael Dahl has written about werewolves, magicians, and superheroes. He loves funny books, scary books, and mysterious books. Every Michael Dahl Presents book is chosen by Michael himself and written by an author he loves. The books are about favorite subjects like legendary myths, haunted houses, farting pigs, or magical powers that go haywire. Read on!

FROM MICHAEL DAHL:

Dear Reader,

When I was a kid, every Saturday at noon I watched "Epic Theater." I wouldn't brush my teeth or take a shower until I had watched an adventure about the secret Sons of Hercules. Hey, I thought, maybe I was a Greek hero in disguise and didn't know it! No such luck. No Medusa showed up at my door, no Hydra terrorized the neighborhood. So, I read every book on mythology in our school library, just in case Zeus sent me on a quest. But then I ran out of stories.

Recently, I asked some terrific authors I know to tell new adventures. They retell the exploits of my favorite heroes, like Hercules and Perseus and Jason, but in a totally different way. A gross and gruesome and disgusting way! Crack open a book from GROSS GODS, and you'll be inspired to be an epic hero. You might also be inspired to take a shower and clean the gunk from between your toes.

READ ON!

Michael Dahl

TABLE OF
CONTENTS

CHAPTER ONE

A DARE

"I got you now, Medusa!" Perseus shouts as he leaps up onto a stool.

Our hero holds his shield in one hand and wields a spear with the other.

On the wall in front of him he has drawn a horrible monster. She has sharp teeth and snakes for hair.

"I won't look into your eyes," he shouts, ducking behind his shield. (That's because the real Medusa can turn anyone she looks at to sludge.)

Perseus lunges with his spear and shouts, "Poke! Poke! Poke!" as he pretends to slay the monster.

Then he stands up on the stool, raising his shield and spear above his head. "I am victorious!" he exclaims.

Suddenly there is a loud **KRAK!** A leg on the stool breaks, and Perseus tumbles to the ground, landing with a **THUD**. His spear goes flying and **THUNKS** into the ceiling. His shield **CRASHES** into a vase, shattering it.

"**PER-SEE-USS!**" his mother shouts from the kitchen. "What have you done?"

His mother, Princess Danaë, storms into the room. She looks at Perseus lying on the floor.

Then she glances at the spear stuck in the ceiling. Her face turns slightly red. Next, she sees the shield and broken vase. Her face grows a little more red. Lastly, she turns to the drawing of Medusa on the wall. And now she is bright red.

"What is that on the wall?" she asks.

"It's Medusa," Perseus says.

"And why does she have yellow talons?" Danaë asks.

"I didn't have any crayons," Perseus explains, digging a finger into his ear. Then he pulls out a yellow glob on the tip of his finger. "So I used earwax to draw her claws."

"Do I want to know why her snaky hair is green?" his mother asks.

"Well . . . ," Perseus begins, digging a pinkie into his nose. Then he pulls out a green blob on the tip of his finger. "I used boogers."

"Instead of drawing on the walls and poking holes in the ceiling and breaking vases," his mother says, "just go on a quest or something."

"A quest?" Perseus says. "But for what?"

"I don't know," his mother shrugs. Then looking back at the picture on the wall, she says, "Why don't you get me one of Medusa's snake hairs."

"Is that a dare?" Perseus asks, sounding interested.

There is nothing a hero like Perseus enjoys more than a dare that leads him on a quest.

"Yes!" Danaë says. "If it will keep you from breaking things!"

CHAPTER TWO

THREE OLD WITCHES

The next day, Perseus completely forgot what he was supposed to do on his quest. Well, that's because our hero is somewhat forgetful. Most days, he is lucky to remember putting on his underpants.

So Perseus sits on his porcelain throne (aka the toilet). That is where he does his best thinking (and remembering). And while there, he also has some business to take care of.

Perseus scrunches up his face and . . .
FFFRRRTTT! That is followed by a loud **PLOP!**

"That sounded like a brownie bomb!" someone says from outside Perseus' stall.

That is followed by a chorus of gasps and giggles.

"I wish it smelled like brownies," someone else says.

"Smells more like broccoli," another someone says.

"Hey, Perseus, what'd you have for breakfast?" the last someone asks.

Perseus opens the stall door to see his hero friends Hercules, Theseus, Jason, and Odysseus. They are playing a game.

On the bathroom mirror, someone has drawn a bull's-eye. The heroes are taking turns flicking blobs of boogers and globs of earwax at it.

"Bull's-eye!" Odysseus shouts as his wad of earwax **SPLATS** in the center circle.

"Want to play?" Hercules, with a finger halfway up his nose, asks Perseus.

"No," Perseus replies. "But you helped me remember that I am going to see Medusa today."

"The snaky-haired woman?" Jason asks.

"But why?" Hercules asks.

"I don't remember," Perseus replies.

"Do you even know where she lives?" Theseus asks.

"I've forgotten that too," Perseus says.

"I bet the three old witches will know," Odysseus says. "They know everything."

The next day, Perseus and his friends head off on an adventure.

They wade through a bottomless bog full of leaches. "Ewww! One slithered up my nose," Theseus whines as Perseus tries to pull it out.

The heroes row across an endless yellow sea.

"Better steer around that big brown log," Jason says.

"I don't think that's a log," Odysseus says.

"Looks more like giant doo-doo," Perseus says.

And they tiptoe through a field of cow pies. **SPLAT!** "Ew! I stepped in one," Theseus says, holding up one foot, which is covered in poo.

Then they finally find a small cave in the middle of a meadow. From inside come loud **CACKLES** and **SCREECHES**.

"That's where the three old hags live," Odysseus says.

The heroes sneak up to the cave and peek inside. The three old hags huddle around a bubbling cauldron.

"I wonder what's for dinner?" Hercules asks.

"Hope it's not broccoli," Jason says.

"I don't think it's dinner," Perseus says. "Look!"

The heroes watch as one of the witches uses a large wooden fork to pull a piece of cloth from the water. The other two witches grab an end of the cloth and stretch it out.

It's a giant pair of underwear! They hang them up to dry.

"Did we get all the skid marks out?" the first witch asks.

"I can't tell," the second witch says.

"Who has the eye?" the third witch cries.

Perseus notices that where their eyes should be, the old hags just have empty eye sockets.

The three old witches begin to dig through the pockets of their ratty robes. Moths and flies flutter about.

The first witch pulls out a large snail from her pocket.

"I think I found it," she screeches as she tries to push the snail into an eye socket. "But it keeps squirming out."

"It's probably just a snail," the third witch cries.

"I think *I* found it," the second witch says, holding up a wad of chewed gum. She sticks it in her eye socket and blinks a couple times. "But I can't see a thing."

"Did you stick gum in your eye again?" the first witch asks.

"Wait . . . I think *I* found it!" the third witch says, holding up an eyeball.

She pops it into her socket and blinks a few times.

"I can see now," the witch says.

Just then, Perscus' friends push him into the cave.

"Don't forget why we're here," Jason says.

Perseus stumbles forward and kicks a loose rock. It goes rolling and bouncing, banging and thudding into the cave.

"Who's there?" the first witch asks.

"Don't be shy," the second witch screeches.

The witch with the eye sees Perseus and cries, "It's one of those Greek heroes!"

"Does he have a spare cyeball?" the first witch asks.

"He has two," the witch with the eye says.

"Then he has one to spare," the second witch says.

Perseus wants to turn and run, but his friends are blocking the way.

"Remember why we're here," Theseus says.

"And why are you here, young man?" the third witch asks.

"I was told you could tell me where Medusa's lair is," Perseus says.

The witches snicker and laugh.

"We can help you," the first witch screeches.

"If you give us an eyeball," the second witch says. She pulls a bent-up spoon out of her pocket and starts to stumble toward Perseus. "Let me just pop one out."

"No, no!" Perseus says, horrified. "I don't have an eye to spare."

"What about a tooth?" the first witch says, smiling to show off her toothless gums.

Where her teeth once were, there are gaping holes filled with purplish puss and squirming maggots.

"I could use a tooth, too," the second witch says, smiling to show off her own toothless gums.

"I still have a tooth," the third witch says, smiling. In her gums is one single rotted tooth. "But could use another one."

She bends down to pick up a rusty pliers and starts to hobble toward Perseus.

"No, no!" Perseus says. "I like my teeth."

"This won't hurt," the witch with the bent-up spoon says.

"Not one bit," the witch with the rusty pliers says.

Perseus isn't sure what to do. He is trapped between a witch who wants to scoop his eyeballs out of their sockets like they were ice cream and another who wants to pluck his teeth from his gums.

That's when he notices the large pair of underwear again.

"Hey, whose underwear is that?" he asks.

"Those belong to Atlas," the first witch screeches.

Atlas is a superstrong Titan. He once angered Zeus by saying the ruler of the gods had a giant butt. So he was punished to help Zeus hold up his humongous heinie for all eternity.

"We do his laundry," the witch wanting to scoop out Perseus' eyeballs says.

"But he never comes to pick it up," the witch wanting to pull out his teeth says.

That gives Perseus an idea.

"I will deliver Atlas' tighty-whities if you help me find Medusa," the hero says.

CHAPTER THREE

ZEUS' BUTT

Perseus climbs up a towering mountain. Behind him are his four friends. Each carries a big bundle on their back.

"This is no fair," Jason groans.

"Why do we have to carry Atlas' underwear?" Theseus moans.

"Because this is my adventure," Perseus says. "It is my job to lead. Not to carry giant skivvies."

"But I'm carrying two pairs," Hercules whines.

"That's because you're the mighty Hercules," Odysseus jokes.

The heroes continue to climb up, up, and up. They crawl through rocky crevasses. They stumble over giant boulders. And they trudge through deep canyons.

When they reach the tallest mountain peak in the world, the heroes find Atlas. He squats and hunches over with his arms spread wide. On his back sits the most humongous heinie they have ever seen. It is Zeus' behind that Atlas is holding up.

"We got your clean underwear for you," Perseus says.

"You brought five pairs?" the Titan asks. "Great! That's a year's supply."

"The witches said you'd tell us where Medusa lives if we brought them to you," Perseus explains.

"First, I need you to change the pair I am wearing now," the Titan says. "Could one of you hold up Zeus' behind while I put on a clean pair?"

The friends all turn to Hercules. "Why me?" he asks.

"Because you're the mighty Hercules," Jason says.

"The strongest man alive," Odysseus adds.

"Only you have the strength to do it!" Perseus says.

"OK, OK," Hercules agrees.

He walks over to Atlas. The Titan lifts up Zeus' behind and plops it down on Hercules' shoulders.

"Oomph!" Hercules grunts. "Could I get some help here?"

Jason and Theseus go over to help Hercules with the humongous rump.

"Just so you know, Zeus had broccoli omelets for breakfast," Atlas says. Then the giant grabs a pair of underwear and walks around a rock to change.

Suddenly, a loud **PPPTTTHHHBBBBBBB!** erupts from Zeus' backside. A green cloud of gas surrounds Hercules. He begins to choke and gag.

"It smells like broccoli!" Perseus coughs.

"And a hint of cheese," Odysseus adds.

Once Atlas has changed his underwear, he rejoins the heroes.

"Are you ready to take Hercules' place?" Perseus asks.

"No," the Titan says, shaking his head. "I'm tired of Zeus' gas . . . especially after taco night!"

"The ruler of the gods sure does like his hot sauce," Hercules grunts.

Meanwhile, the gas cloud surrounding Hercules and Jason grows thicker every time Zeus **FFFRRRTTTS** or **TTTHHHPPPPS**.

"I can't breathe," Hercules chokes.

"I can't see," Jason cries.

"OK, OK," Perseus says to the Titan. "Just tells us where we can find Medusa."

"You will find her that way, in the rotting forest," the Titan says pointing into the distance.

Then the giant starts to walk away.

"But wait a second," Perseus pleads. "Could you do us one favor?"

"What is it?" Atlas asks.

"We let you change your underwear," Perseus begins. "Could you let Hercules change his before you leave?"

"Um . . . sure," the Titan grunts. He walks over to Zeus' behind and picks it up off of Hercules' shoulder and puts it on his. "Just hurry up."

"OK, everyone. Let's get out of here," Perseus says.

The heroes run off.

"Hey, you tricked me!" Atlas shouts.

But it is too late. The heroes are already climbing down the mountain.

CHAPTER FOUR

THE ROTTING FOREST

Perseus and his friends quickly scamper down the mountainside. Behind them, Atlas' curses grow more and more distant.

Then the heroes begin to trek across a dry and dusty desert. Sand is everywhere. It gets in their eyes. It covers their hair. They breathe it in and **COUGH** and **CHOKE**.

"Are you sure we're going the right way?" Jason asks.

"Yes," Perseus replies.

"Really?" Hercules asks. "All I see is sand. It's crusting over my eyeballs."

"Really," Perseus says, sounding a little annoyed.

"But did you remember which way Atlas said to go?" Theseus asks.

"Yes, this way," Perseus grunts, starting to sound mad.

"Really?" Odysseus asks. "It feels like I'm swallowing sandpaper."

"She lives in there!" Perseus shouts.

In front of the heroes, the desert ends suddenly. Beyond is a forest of towering trees.

"Sure that's not a mirage?" Odysseus asks.

"Do mirages smell like fungus and rotting spinach?" Perseus asks.

The smell coming from the forest is horrible, and the trees do not look like any they have seen before. All of their branches sag toward the ground. The leaves on those branches are brown and moldy.

"Everything is rotting," Jason says.

"It's because of Medusa," Perseus says. "Everything she looks at begins to rot."

As the heroes wind their way through the forest, the ground squishes underneath their feet. Globs of moldy leaves **SPLAT** and **SPLUNK** all about.

But that's not all. As they walk, giant slugs slither over their feet. Huge flies **BUZZ** about their heads, and giant beetles **SNAP** at them from the trees.

After walking for a while, they spot a rundown hut in a clearing. Mold grows on its walls and mushrooms stick out of its roof.

"That must be where Medusa lives," Perseus says. He starts to sneak up to the hut but then notices that his friends aren't following. "Aren't you coming?" he asks them.

"But why are we here?" Hercules asks.

"We lugged giant underwear up a mountain," Jason says. "And held up Zeus' backside."

"And trekked through a disgusting rotting forest," Theseus adds.

"But what for?" Odysseus adds. "Why do you need to see Medusa?"

Perseus wishes he had his porcelain throne right now. Not because our hero has to take care of business, but so he could think—and remember. He was on this quest because of his mother. That much he does remember.

"My mother was annoyed with me for some reason," Perseus tells his friends.

"Were you playing with your spear in the house again?" Jason asks.

"Remember that time you accidently poked your dad in the tush?" Theseus laughs.

And that is when our hero remembers why he is on this quest. His tells his friends about poking a hole in the ceiling with his spear and then breaking a vase with his shield.

"And then my mother said, 'Why don't you go on a quest to pluck out one of Medusa's snake hairs,'" Perseus tells his friends.

"So it was a dare!" Hercules says.

"Then let's go get one of Medusa's stinky snakes!" Jason shouts.

The heroes sneak up to the entrance of the hut. Inside, they see Medusa sitting on a bench and eating dinner. In front of her, there is a heaping plate of broccoli. But as she eats, her dinner slowly rots.

The broccoli wilts and turns from green to brown. Then it begins to ooze grayish goo.

Medusa picks up a gooey piece. "Just how I like it," she says. "Extra slimy."

She slurps it up and begins to chew.

"That smells worse than Zeus' farts," Hercules says.

"And you should know," Theseus adds.

"Shhh, we don't want her to know we are here," Perseus whispers.

As they watch Medusa eat, Perseus notices that her hair moves and slithers. When some of the broccoli goo squirts out from between Medusa's jagged teeth, a strand of it stands up like a snake. It snatches the goo out of the air.

Perseus knows he can't have Medusa look at him. Otherwise he will be turned into a pile of stinking sludge. So as he sneaks into the hut, he holds his shield in front of him.

When he is right behind her, he reaches up to grab up one of her snake hairs. But . . .

"OW!" he screams. "It bit me."

One of the snake hairs has latched onto the tip of his finger.

As Medusa jumps up, Perseus yanks his finger away, but the snake does not let go.

PLUCK! And he pulls it right out of Medusa's head.

"Ow! That hurt!" Medusa screams. "For that, I am going to turn you into sludge with my cursed gaze."

Perseus holds up his shield, so at least Medusa is not looking directly at him.

But Medusa is looking at something. Perseus' shield begins to wilt and ooze and become gooey.

"Ew, it's like I'm holding a giant loogy," he yells to his friends.

Then he notices that they are no longer there. They are already running away.

Tossing his shield aside, Perseus turns away and runs after his friends.

CHAPTER FIVE

THE CHASE HOME

"Come back with my stinky snake!"
Medusa yells.

Perseus keeps running. He tries to shake
the snake loose from the tip of his finger,
but the nasty little bugger won't let go. Being
bitten by a stinky snake, he has decided,
is better than getting turned to goo by an
angry monster.

So he runs.

Perseus runs as fast as he can. His friends are just ahead of him doing the same.

Hercules darts through swarms of buzzing flies.

BUZZ! BUZZ! BUZZ!

Jason leaps over a mound of slithering slugs.

SLITHER! SLITHER! SLITHER!

Theseus ducks under a snapping beetle.

SNAP! SNAP! SNAP!

Odysseus dodges moldy globs dropping from a tree.

GLOP! GLOP! GLOP!

As Perseus runs, he feels something strange happening to his clothes. First his boots begin to turn into brown goop. It feels like he is wearing soggy mushrooms on his feet.

Then his shirt and his pants begin to ooze. It feels like he is covered in slime from head to toe.

He knows it is because of Medusa. Her power is rotting his clothes. And he knows that he can't look back at her. Otherwise he would be turned to sludge too.

Perseus and his friends burst out of the rotting forest. They quickly begin crossing the desert.

The running becomes difficult, because Medusa's power is even causing the sand to turn into muck.

But then they reach the mountain. They climb up and up, never daring to look back.

At the top, they spy Atlas holding up Zeus' butt. He is surrounded in a cloud of orange gas.

"Do I smell refried beans?" Theseus says.

"What did Zeus have for lunch?" Jason stops to ask Atlas. But Perseus pulls him along.

"Keep running," Perseus says. "We can't let Medusa catch up to us."

The heroes tiptoe through the cow pie fields.

SPLAAAAAAAAT!

"Why does that always happen to me?" Theseus says, limping along with a poo-covered foot.

Then they cross the yellow sea, leaping from one big brown stinking log to the next big brown stinking log.

Lastly, they wade through the bottomless bog of leeches.

"I am covered with them," Hercules whines, as thick black leeches dangle from his nose, his arms, and his legs.

All the while, the heroes never look back. They don't dare. And they don't stop running until they reach Perseus' house.

They dash inside and duck behind a couch.

"Is she still following us?" Jason asks.

"I don't dare look," Theseus says.

Then the heroes notice something frightening. All the plants in the house begin to wilt.

"She's here," Odysseus says.

"She's causing the plants to die," Hercules adds.

As they are wondering what to do next, Perseus' mother steps into the room. A stinky haze surrounds her. She winces at the smell.

"Whoa! It's not Medusa causing the plants to wilt," she says.

Perseus' mother points at the totally disgusting heroes. "It's you!" she says. "You all reek like you bathed in sewage stew and then were blow-dried with ogre farts."

The heroes all let out a sigh.

"Now if I could just get this stinking snake to stop biting me," Perseus whines, shaking his finger. "My quest would be complete."

THE REAL MYTH

In Greek myths, Perseus was the son of Princess Danaë and Zeus, ruler of the gods.

Perseus grew up on the island of Seriphus. Its ruler, King Polydectes, wanted to marry Danaë. When Perseus attempted to stop him, Polydectes dared the young hero to bring back the head of Medusa.

Medusa was a horrible monster with snakes for hair. She was so frightening that anyone who gazed into her eyes was turned to stone.

Perseus had help on his quest. He was given winged sandals, a sword, and a bronze shield by the gods to help him on his quest. To find Medusa's lair, Perseus visited the Graeae. These three witches had one eye and one tooth that they shared and were sisters of Medusa. They told Perseus that Atlas could tell him where to find Medusa.

Atlas sent Perseus to the end of the world, to Medusa's lair.

Perseus couldn't look at the horrible monster, or he would be turned to stone. Instead, he used the bronze shield as a mirror to find Medusa. Then he cut off her head.

Afterward, Perseus returned to Seriphus with Medusa's head. He showed it to Polydectes and turned the king to stone. His mother was saved!

GLOSSARY

eternity (ih-TUR-net-ee)—endless time or forever

heinie (HY-nee)—another word for butt or backside

porcelain throne (POR-suh-len THRONE)—another word for toilet

quest (KWEST)—a journey made to find something or to perform a task

talons—(TAL-uhn) the claw of an animal and especially of a bird of prey

Titan (TYTE-uhn)—one of a family of giants overthrown by the gods of ancient Greece

scamper (SKAM-puhr)— to run lightly and usually playfully about

skivvies (SKIV-eez)—another word for underwear

Zeus (ZOOS)—chief god, ruler of the sky and weather, and husband of Hera in Greek mythology

AUTHOR

Blake Hoena grew up in central Wisconsin, where he wrote stories about robots conquering the moon and trolls lumbering around the woods behind his parents' house. He now lives in St. Paul, Minnesota, and continues to make up stories about things like space aliens and superheroes, and he has written more than 70 chapter books and graphic novels for children.

ILLUSTRATOR

Ivica Stevanovic is an illustrator, comic artist, and graphic designer. He has published a huge number of illustrations in schoolbooks and picture books. Apart from working on illustrations for children's books, Ivica draws comics, and his specialty is graphic novels. His best-known graphic novel is *Kindly Corpses*. Ivica lives with his wife Milica and their two daughters Katarina and Teodora in Veternik (Serbia).

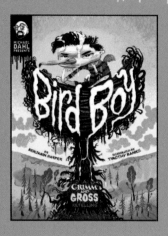
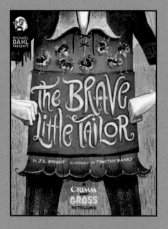
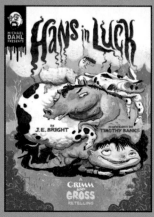